HAMISH THE HEDGEHOG
The Kitchen Critter

Written by P.J. Tierney

Illustrated by Aishwarya Vohra

For Julia Rose Tierney, Hamish's first supporter
and much appreciated creative collaborator.
You are amazing, and I can't wait to see all you become.
A big Hamish Hedgie Hug to you!

Printed in the United States of America

Typography by Wilsted & Taylor Publishing Services

Library of Congress Cataloging-in-Publication data is available.
ISBN 978-1-943016-10-5

First Edition
24 23 22 21 20   10 9 8 7 6 5 4 3 2 1

Kitchen Ink Publishing
114 John Street, #277
New York, NY 10038

Kitchen Ink books may be purchased for educational, business, or sales promotional use. For information, please email the Special Markets Department at sales@kitcheninkpublishing.com.

See what Kitchen Ink is up to, share recipes and tips, and shop our store—
www.kitcheninkpublishing.com.

Follow the real Hamish's adventures on Instagram: Hamish_thehedgehog.

Hamish the hedgehog taught
himself to make baskets using twigs
he found around his forest home.

One morning while picking berries, Hamish smelled something sweet, and he couldn't resist following this delicious smell to a house at the edge of the woods.

Hamish walked toward the house and stood
on a tree stump. Through the window he
saw a kitchen table set for breakfast.

Hamish walked back
into the woods, leaving his
basket of berries behind.

The next day Hamish found a basket of berry muffins with a recipe on the tree stump. How Hamish wished he knew how to cook. He had never eaten berry muffins, and they looked delicious!

VERY BERRY MUFFINS

Ingredients

1 1/2 Cups All-Purpose Flour

3/4 Cup Sugar

2 tsp. Baking Powder

1/2 tsp. Salt

1/2 Cup Milk

2 Large Eggs, Well Beaten

1/4 Cup Butter, Melted

1 tsp. Vanilla Extract

1 Cup Raspberries

1 Cup Blueberries

Recipe

1. Preheat oven to 375° F. Fill 12 muffin cups with paper liners or spray with nonstick spray.

2. In a large bowl, mix flour, sugar, baking powder, and salt.

3. In a medium bowl, whisk together milk, eggs, melted butter, and vanilla.

4. Pour wet ingredients into dry ingredients and mix gently, until just combined, being careful not to overmix.

5. Gently fold blueberries and raspberries into batter.

6. Fill muffin cups two-thirds full. Bake for 15 to 20 minutes, until golden brown on top and a toothpick inserted into center of muffin comes out clean.

MAKES 12 MUFFINS

Hamish returned to the house and
left a basket full of strawberries with
a thank-you note on the tree stump.

Each morning Hamish left a basket of something from the forest and returned to the woods with a basket of something delicious. The family would wait at the window, watching and smiling.

Strawberry Cupcakes and Frosting

Ingredients: Cake

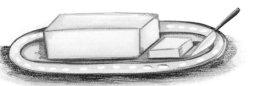

1/2 Cup Butter, Softened

1 Cup Sugar

2 Eggs

2 tsp. Vanilla

1 1/2 Cups Flour

1 1/4 tsp. Baking Powder

1/4 tsp. Salt

1 Cup Fresh Strawberries, Chopped

Ingredients: Frosting

1/2 Cup Butter, Softened

4 Oz. Cream Cheese, Softened

1 tsp. Vanilla

1-2 tsp. Milk

4 1/2 Cups Powdered Sugar

Recipe

1. Preheat oven to 350° F. Fill 12 muffin cups with paper liners or spray with nonstick spray.

2. In a large bowl, beat butter and sugar until light and fluffy.

3. Add eggs and vanilla and beat until well combined.

4. Add flour, baking powder, and salt and mix well.

5. Add chopped strawberries and stir for 1 to 2 minutes, until strawberries begin to break down.*

6. Fill paper liners two-thirds full. Bake for 15 to 20 minutes, or until a toothpick inserted in center of cupcake comes out clean.

*For sweeter cupcakes add 1 tablespoon strawberry jam.

FROSTING

1. While cupcakes are cooling, beat butter and cream cheese together until smooth.

2. Beat in vanilla and milk, and then add powdered sugar to desired consistency.

3. Frost each cupcake.

MAKES
12 CUPCAKES

Everyone loved the cupcakes.

Not everyone loved the fruit roll-ups.

BLACKBERRY FRUIT ROLL-UPS

Ingredients

1 Pint Blackberries

1 tsp. Lime Juice

1/4 Cup Honey

Recipe

1. Preheat oven to 170° F. Line a rimmed baking sheet with parchment paper.

2. Puree blackberries, lime juice, and honey in a blender or food processor until smooth.

3. Pour mixture onto baking sheet and spread evenly with a spatula. Bake for 5 to 6 hours, or until completely dried out but still sticky.

4. Remove pan from oven and allow to cool for at least 30 minutes.

5. Cut mixture into long strips. Start at one end and roll up each strip. Store in airtight container.

Mushroom Lentil Veggie Burger Sliders

Ingredients

2 tbl. Coconut Oil

4 Garlic Cloves, Minced

1 Shallot, Chopped

3 Cups Raw Mushrooms, Chopped

1 Cup Cooked Lentils

1 Cup Raw Walnut Halves

1 tbl. Soy Sauce

2 tsp. Cumin Powder

1 tsp. Turmeric

1 tsp. Salt

1 Pinch Black Pepper

10 Slider Rolls, Split

Tomato Slices

Lettuce

Sliced Onion

Pickles

Recipe

1. Preheat oven to 375° F. Line a baking sheet with parchment paper.

2. In a large skillet, heat 1 tablespoon coconut oil until melted. Add garlic and shallots and sauté until shallots are translucent.

3. Add chopped mushrooms and other tablespoon of coconut oil and sauté until mushrooms are fully cooked. Set aside to cool.

4. Pulse walnut halves in a food processor until they reach a flour-like consistency.

5. Add lentils, mushrooms, soy sauce, cumin, turmeric, salt, and pepper to walnuts. Blend until smooth, leaving some chunks of lentils and mushrooms.

6. Form 10 equal-sized patties and place on baking sheet. Bake for 20 to 25 minutes, until burgers are lightly browned on top.

7. Serve on slider rolls with toppings of your choice, like tomato, lettuce, onion, and pickles.

MAKES 10 SLIDERS

The animals were having a ball
and had never eaten so well.

Crunchy Baked Asparagus

Ingredients

1 Cup Panko Bread Crumbs

1/2 Cup Grated Parmesan Cheese

2 Large Eggs

1/4 Cup All-Purpose Flour

Pepper to Taste

1 Pound Asparagus

Recipe

1. Preheat oven to 425° F and grease a baking sheet.
2. Combine Panko and Parmesan cheese in a resealable bag and put flour into another bag.
3. Beat two eggs in a shallow bowl.
4. Place asparagus in flour bag and shake to coat.
5. Remove asparagus from flour and dip into eggs.
6. Put asparagus into bread crumb bag and shake until well coated.
7. Arrange asparagus in a single layer on greased baking sheet and bake for 10 to 12 minutes, or until golden brown and crisp.

MAKES 12–18, DEPENDING ON SIZE

One morning, Hamish found a note in the empty basket on the stump.

Hamish, please join us for dinner tomorrow at 6pm.

The Nolan family.

He left his basket of dandelions and skipped back into the forest, excited but unsure of what to bring to dinner.

Hamish wanted to bring a gift to dinner. He needed the perfect pieces of wood—and he needed to work quickly.

Hamish told his friends about his invitation.
Everyone was happy for him, and as he walked away
Otter yelled, "Don't forget to bring back leftovers!"

As Hamish rang the doorbell, he could smell all sorts of deliciousness. He was greeted by the Nolans and presented the salad tongs.

"Well, then, you are going to need this hat and
apron for our cooking classes," his friends said.
"And right now, you can help frost the cake!"

Chocolate Cake With Vanilla Frosting

INGREDIENTS : CAKE

3/4 Cup
Cocoa Powder
(Unsweetened)

1 3/4 Cups
All- Purpose Flour

1 1/2 tsp.
Baking Powder

1 1/2 tsp.
Baking Soda

2 Cups White Sugar

1 tsp. Salt

2 Eggs

1 Cup Milk
(Low or Full fat)

1/2 Cup
Vegetable Oil
(or Canola)

2 tsp. Vanilla
Extract

1 Cup Boiling Water

INGREDIENTS : FROSTING

1 Cup Butter, Softened
(2 Sticks)

3-4 Cups
Confectioners'
Sugar (Sifted)

2 tsp. Vanilla

Pinch Salt

2-3 tbl.
Milk, Heavy Cream,
or Half-and-Half

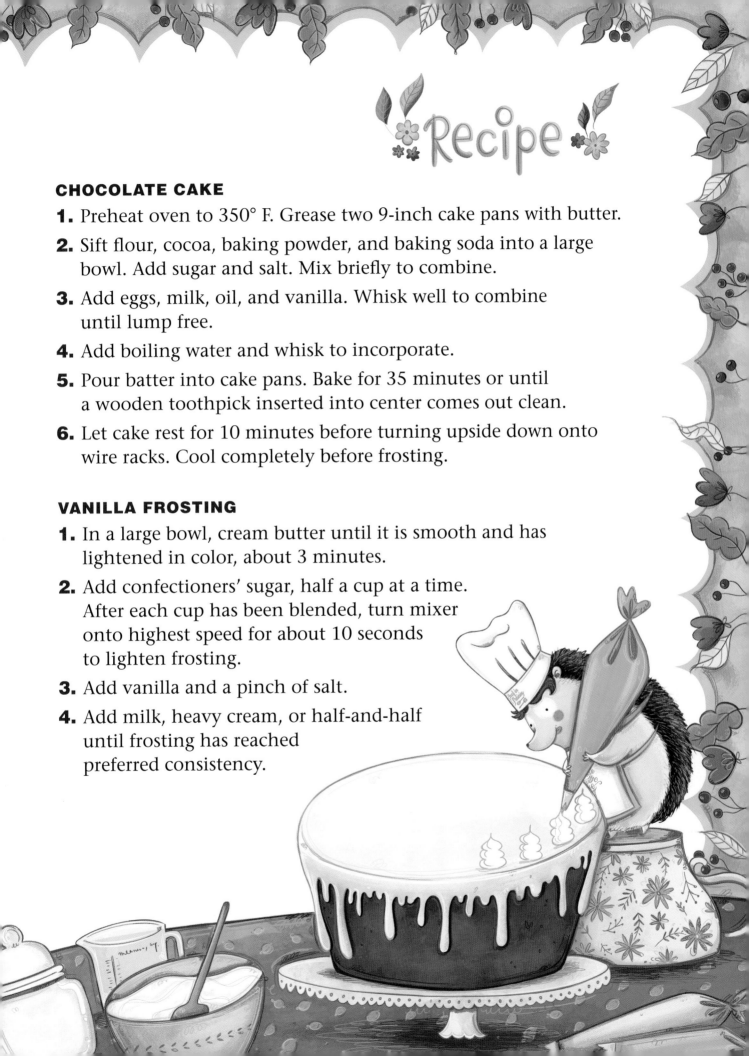

Recipe

CHOCOLATE CAKE

1. Preheat oven to 350° F. Grease two 9-inch cake pans with butter.

2. Sift flour, cocoa, baking powder, and baking soda into a large bowl. Add sugar and salt. Mix briefly to combine.

3. Add eggs, milk, oil, and vanilla. Whisk well to combine until lump free.

4. Add boiling water and whisk to incorporate.

5. Pour batter into cake pans. Bake for 35 minutes or until a wooden toothpick inserted into center comes out clean.

6. Let cake rest for 10 minutes before turning upside down onto wire racks. Cool completely before frosting.

VANILLA FROSTING

1. In a large bowl, cream butter until it is smooth and has lightened in color, about 3 minutes.

2. Add confectioners' sugar, half a cup at a time. After each cup has been blended, turn mixer onto highest speed for about 10 seconds to lighten frosting.

3. Add vanilla and a pinch of salt.

4. Add milk, heavy cream, or half-and-half until frosting has reached preferred consistency.